Roberto Bolaño
Antwerp

TRANSLATED BY NATASHA WIMMER

Roberto Bolaño (1953–2003) was the author of *The Savage Detectives* and *2666*, among many other notable works. Born in Santiago, Chile, he later lived in Mexico City, Paris, and Barcelona. His accolades include the National Book Critics Circle Award and the Premio Rómulo Gallegos. He died at the age of fifty and is widely considered to be the greatest Latin American writer of his generation.

Natasha Wimmer is a translator of contemporary fiction and literary nonfiction. She is a regular visiting lecturer at Princeton University and Columbia University and she has written reviews and criticism for *The New York Times* and *The New York Review of Books*, among other publications.

T0268698

Also by Roberto Bolaño

Antwerp

Roberto Bolaño

Antwerp

Translated from the Spanish by
NATASHA WIMMER

Picador
New York

Picador
120 Broadway, New York 10271

Printed in the United States of America
Originally published in 2002 by Editorial Anagrama, Spain, as *Amberes*
English translation originally published in 2010 by New Directions,
by arrangement with the Heirs of Roberto Bolaño and Carmen
Balcells Agencia Literaria, Barcelona
First Picador paperback edition, 2024

The Pascal epigraph is taken from A. J. Krailsheimer's translation for the
Penguin Classics edition, slightly altered.

Library of Congress Cataloging-in Publication Data
Names: Bolaño, Roberto, 1953–2003, author. | Wimmer, Natasha, translator.
Title: Antwerp / Roberto Bolaño ; translated from the Spanish by Natasha
    Wimmer.
Other titles: Amberes. English
Description: First Picador paperback edition. | New York : Picador, 2024.
Identifiers: LCCN 2024019040 | ISBN 9781250898166 (paperback)
Subjects: LCGFT: Experimental fiction. | Novellas.
Classification: LCC PQ8098.12.O38 A6313 2024 | DDC 863/.64—dc23/eng/20240503
LC record available at https://lccn.loc.gov/2024019040

Designed by Erik Rieselbach

D   10   9   8   7   6   5   4   3   2

for Alexandra Bolaño and Lautaro Bolaño

TOTAL ANARCHY:
TWENTY-TWO YEARS LATER

I wrote this book for myself, and even that I can't be sure of. For a long time these were just loose pages that I reread and maybe tinkered with, convinced I had no *time*. But time for what? I couldn't say exactly. I wrote this book for the ghosts, who, because they're outside of time, are the only ones with time. After the last rereading (just now), I realize that time isn't the only thing that matters, time isn't the only source of terror. Pleasure can be terrifying too, and so can courage. In those days, if memory serves, I lived exposed to the elements, without my papers, the way other people live in castles. I never brought this novel to any publishing house, of course. They would've slammed the door in my face and I'd have lost the copy. I didn't even make what's technically termed a clean copy. The original manuscript has more pages: the text tended to multiply itself, spreading like a sickness. My sickness, back then, was pride, rage, and violence. Those things (rage, violence) are exhausting and I spent my days uselessly tired. I worked at night. During the day I wrote and read. I never slept. To keep awake, I drank coffee and smoked. Naturally, I met interesting people, some of them the product of my own hallucinations. I think it was my last year in Barcelona. The scorn I felt for so-called official literature was great, though only a little greater than my scorn for marginal literature. But I believed in literature:

or rather, I didn't believe in arrivisme or opportunism or the whispering of sycophants. I did believe in vain gestures, I did believe in fate. I didn't have children yet. I was still reading more poetry than prose. In those years (or months), I was drawn to certain science fiction writers and certain pornographers, sometimes antithetical authors, as if the cave and the electric light were mutually exclusive. I read Norman Spinrad, James Tiptree, Jr. (whose real name was Alice Sheldon), Restif de la Bretonne, and de Sade. I also read Cervantes and the archaic Greek poets. When I got sick I reread Manrique. One night I came up with a scheme to make money outside the law. A small criminal enterprise. The basic idea was not to get rich too fast. My first accomplice or attempt at an accomplice, a terribly sad Argentinean friend, responded to my scheme with a saying that went something like this: if you have to be in prison or in the hospital, then the best place to be is your own country, for the visitors, I guess. His response didn't have the slightest effect on me, because I felt equally distant from all the countries in the world. Later I gave up my plan when I discovered that it was worse than working in a brick factory. Tacked up over my bed was a piece of paper on which I'd asked a friend from Poland to write, in Polish, "Total Anarchy." I didn't think I was going to live past thirty-five. I was happy. Then came 1981, and before I knew it, everything had changed.

BLANES, 2002

When I consider the brief span of my life absorbed into the eternity which comes before and after—*memoria hospitis unius diei praetereuntis*—the small space I occupy and which I see swallowed up in the infinite immensity of spaces of which I know nothing and which know nothing of me, I take fright and am amazed to see myself here rather than there: there is no reason for me to be here rather than there, now rather than then. Who put me here? By whose command and act were this place and time allotted to me?

—PASCAL

Antwerp

Antwerp

1. FACADE

Once photographed, life here is ended. It is almost symbolic of Hollywood. Tara has no rooms inside. It was just a facade.

—DAVID O. SELZNICK

The kid heads toward the house. Alley of larches. The Fronde. Necklace of tears. Love is a mix of sentimentality and sex (Burroughs). The mansion is just a facade—dismantled, to be erected in Atlanta. 1959. Everything looks worn. Not a recent phenomenon. From a long time back, everything wrecked. And the Spaniards imitate the way you talk. The South American lilt. An alley of palms. Everything slow and asthmatic. Bored biologists watch the rain from the windows of their corporations. It's no good singing *with feeling*. My darling, wherever you are: it's too late, forget the gesture that never came. "It was just a facade." The kid walks toward the house.

2. THE FULLNESS OF THE WIND

Twin highways flung across the evening, when everything seems to indicate that memory and finer feelings are kaput, like the rental car of a tourist who unknowingly ventures into war zones and never returns, at least not by car, a man who speeds down highways strung across a zone that his mind refuses to accept as a barrier, vanishing point (the transparent dragon), and in the news Sophie Podolski is kaput in Belgium, the girl from the Montfaucon Research Center (a smell unbefitting a woman), and the spent lips say "I see waiters, hired for the summer, walking along a deserted beach at eight o'clock at night" ... "Slow movements, real or unreal I don't know" ... "A sandswept group" ... "For an instant, a fat eleven-year-old girl lit up the public pool" ... "So is Colan Yar after you too?" ... "The highway, a black-topped strip of prairie?" ... The man sits at one of the cafes in the hypothetical ghetto. He writes postcards because breathing prevents him from writing the poems he'd like to write. I mean: free poems, no extra tax. His eyes retain a vision of naked bodies coming slowly out of the sea. Then all that's left is emptiness. "Waiters walking along the beach" ... "The evening light dismantles our sense of the wind" ...

3. GREEN, RED, AND WHITE CHECKS

Now he, or half of him, rises up on a tide. The tide is white. He has taken a train going in the wrong direction. He's the only one in the compartment, the curtains are open, and the dusk clings to the dirty glass. Swift, dark, intense colors unfurl across the black leather of the seats. We've created a silent space so that he can work somehow. He lights a ciga-rette. The box of matches is sepia-colored. On the lid is a drawing of a hexagon made of twelve matches. It's labeled "Playing with Matches," and, as indicated by a 2 in the upper lefthand corner, it's the second game in a series. This game is called "The Great Triangle Escape." Now his attention comes to rest on a pale object. After a while he realizes that it's a square that's beginning to disintegrate. What he at first imagined was a screen becomes a white tide, white words, panes whose transparency is replaced by a blind and perma-nent whiteness. Suddenly a shout focuses his attention. The brief sound is like a color swallowed by a crack. But what color? The phrase "The train stopped in a northern town" distracts him from a shifting of shadows in the next seat. He covers his face with his fingers, spread wide enough so that he can spot any object coming at him. He searches for cigarettes in the pockets of his jacket. With the first puff, it occurs to him that monogamy moves with the same rigid-ity as the train. A cloud of opaline smoke covers his face. It occurs to him that the word "face" creates its own blue eyes.

Someone shouts. He looks at his feet planted on the floor. The word "shoes" will never levitate. He sighs, turning his face to the window. A darker light seems to have settled over the land. Like the light in my head, he thinks. The train is running along the edge of a forest. In some spots, traces of recent fires are visible. He isn't surprised not to see anyone on the edge of the forest. But this is where the little hunchback lives, down a bicycle path, a few miles deeper in. I told him I'd heard enough. There are rabbits and rats here that look like squirrels. The forest is bordered by the highway to the west and the railroad tracks to the east. Nearby there are gardens and tilled fields, and, closer to the city, a polluted river lined with junkyards and gypsy camps. Beyond that is the sea. The hunchback opens a can of food, resting his hump against a small, rotted pine. Someone shouted at the other end of the car, possibly a woman, he said to himself as he stubbed the cigarette out against the sole of his shoe. His shirt is long-sleeved, cotton, with green, red, and white checks. The hunchback holds a can of sardines in tomato sauce in his left hand. He's eating. His eyes scan the foliage. He hears the train go by.

4. I'M MY OWN BEWITCHMENT

The ghosts of the Plaza Real are on the stairs. Blankets pulled up to my ears, motionless in bed, sweating and repeating meaningless words to myself, I hear them moving around, turning the lights on and off, climbing up toward the roof with unbearable slowness. I'm the moon, someone ventures. But I used to be in a gang and I had the Arab in my sights and I pulled the trigger at the worst possible moment. Narrow streets in the heart of Distrito V, and no way to escape or alter the fate that slid like a djellaba over my greasy hair. Words that drift away from one another. Urban games played from time immemorial . . . "Frankfurt" . . . "A blond girl at the biggest window of the boarding house" . . . "There's nothing I can do now" . . . I'm my own bewitchment. My hands move over a mural in which someone, eight inches taller than me, stands in the shadows, hands in the pockets of his jacket, preparing for death and his subsequent transparency. The language of others is unintelligible to me. "Tired after being up for days" . . . "A blond girl came down the stairs" . . . "My name is Roberto Bolaño" . . . "I opened my arms" . . .

5. BLUE

The Calabria Commune campground, according to a sensationalistic article in PEN. Harassed by the townspeople: inside, the campers walked around naked. Six kids dead in the surrounding area. "They were campers" . . . "Not from around here, that's for sure" . . . Months before, the Anti-Terrorist Brigade paid them a visit. "They were out of control, I mean, screwing all over the place: they screwed in groups and wherever they felt like it" . . . "At first they kept to themselves, they only did it at the campground, but this year they had orgies on the beach and right outside town" . . . The police questioning the locals: "I didn't do it," says one, "if somebody had set fire to that place, you could blame me, it's crossed my mind more than once, but I don't have the heart to shoot six kids" . . . Maybe it was the mafia. Maybe they committed suicide. Maybe it was all a dream. The wind in the rocks. The Mediterranean. Blue.

6. REASONABLE PEOPLE VS. UNREASONABLE PEOPLE

"They suspected me from the beginning" ... "Pale men could see what was hidden in the landscape" ... "A campground, a forest, a tennis club, a riding school—the road will take you far away if you want to go far away" ... "They suspected I was a spy but what kind of fucking spy" ... "Reasonable people vs. unreasonable people" ... "That guy running around here doesn't exist" ... "He's the real ringleader of all this" ... "But I also dreamed of girls" ... "People we know, the same faces from last summer" ... "The same kindness" ... "Now time erases all that" ... "The perfect girl suspected me from the very beginning" ... "Something I made up" ... "There was no spying or any shit like that" ... "It was so obvious that they refused to believe it" ...

7. THE NILE

The hell to come . . . Sophie Podolski killed herself years ago . . . She would've been twenty-seven now, like me . . . Egyptian designs on the ceiling, the workers slowly approach, dusty fields, it's the end of April and they're paid in heroin . . . I've turned on the radio, an impersonal voice gives the city-by-city count of those arrested today . . . "Midnight, nothing to report" . . . A girl who wrote dragons, completely fucking sick of it all in some corner of Brussels . . . "Assault rifles, guns, old grenades" . . . I'm alone, all the literary shit gradually falling by the wayside—poetry journals, limited editions, the whole dreary joke behind me now . . . The door opened at the first kick and the guy jammed the gun under your chin . . . Abandoned buildings in Barcelona, almost an invitation to kill yourself in peace . . . The sun on the Nile behind the curtain of dust at sunset . . . The boss pays in heroin and the farm workers snort it in the furrows, on blankets, under scrawled palm trees that someone edits away . . . A Belgian girl who wrote like a star . . . "She would've been twenty-seven now, like me" . . .

8. CLEANING UTENSILS

All praise to the highways and to these moments. Umbrellas abandoned by bums in shopping plazas with white supermarkets rising at the far ends. It's summer and the policemen are drinking at the back of the bar. Next to the jukebox a girl listens to the latest hits. Around the same time, someone is walking, far from here, away from here, with no plans to come back. A naked boy sitting outside his tent in the woods? The girl stumbled into the bathroom and began to vomit. When you think about it, we're not allotted much time here on Earth to make lives for ourselves: I mean, to scrape something together, get married, wait for death. Her eyes in the mirror like letters fanned out in a dark room; the huddled breathing shape burrowed into bed with her. The men talk about dead small-time crooks, the price of houses on the coast, extra paychecks. One day I'll die of cancer. Cleaning utensils begin to levitate in her head. She says: I could go on and on. The kid came into the room and grabbed her by the shoulders. The two of them wept like characters from different movies projected on the same screen. Red scene of bodies turning on the gas. The bony beautiful hand turned the knob. Choose just one of these phrases: "I escaped torture" ... "An unknown hotel" ... "No more roads" ...

9. A MONKEY

To name is to praise, said the girl (eighteen, a poet, long hair). The hour of the ambulance parked in the alley. The medic stubbed out his cigarette on his shoe, then lumbered forward like a bear. I wish those miserable people in the windows would turn out the lights and go to sleep. Who was the first human being to look out a window? (Applause.) People are tired, it wouldn't surprise me if one of these days they greeted us with a hail of bullets. I guess a monkey. I can't string two words together. I can't express myself coherently or write what I want. I should probably give up everything and go away, isn't that what Teresa of Avila did? (Applause and laughter.) A monkey looking out a putrid window, watching the daylight fade. The medic came over to where the sergeant was smoking; they gave each other a slight nod without making eye contact. It was clear at a glance that he hadn't died of a heart attack. He was face down and you could see the bullet holes in his back, in his brown sweater. They emptied a machine gun into him, said a dwarf who was standing to the left of the sergeant and whom the medic hadn't seen. In the distance they heard the muted sounds of a protest march. We'd better go before they block the street, said the dwarf. The sergeant didn't seem to hear him, sunk in contemplation of the dark windows from which people were watching the spectacle. Let's hurry. But where do we go? There aren't any police stations. To name is to praise, said the girl, laughing. The same passion, taken to infinity. Cars stop between potholes and garbage cans. Doors that open and then close for no apparent reason. Engines, streetlights, the ambulance reverses away. The hour swells, bursts. I guess it was a monkey at the top of a tree.

10. THERE WAS NOTHING

There are no police stations, no hospitals, nothing. At least there's nothing money can buy. "We act on instantaneous impulses" . . . "This is the kind of thing that destroys the unconscious, and then we'll be left hanging" . . . "Remember that joke about the bullfighter who steps out into the ring and there's no bull, no ring, nothing?" . . . The policemen drank anarchic breezes. Someone started to clap.

11. AMONG THE HORSES

I dreamed of a woman with no mouth, says the man in bed. I couldn't help smiling. The piston forces the images up again. Look, he tells her, I know another story that's just as sad. He's a writer who lives on the edge of town. He makes a living working at a riding school. He's never asked for much, all he needs is a room and time to read. But one day he meets a girl who lives in another city and he falls in love. They decide to get married. The girl will come to live with him. The first problem arises: finding a place big enough for the two of them. The second problem is where to get the money to pay for it. Then one thing leads to another: a job with a steady income (at the stables he works on commission, plus room, board, and a small monthly stipend), getting his papers in order, registering with social security, etc. But for now, he needs money to get to the city where his fiancée lives. A friend suggests the possibility of writing articles for a magazine. He calculates that the first four would pay for the bus trip there and back and maybe a few days at a cheap hotel. He writes his girlfriend to tell her he's coming. But he can't finish a single article. He spends the evenings sitting outdoors at the bar of the riding school where he works, trying to write, but he can't. Nothing comes out, as they say in common parlance. The man realizes that he's finished. All he writes are short crime stories. The trip recedes from his future, is lost, and he remains listless, inert, going automatically about his work among the horses.

12. THE INSTRUCTIONS

With instructions in an envelope, I left the city. I didn't have far to go, maybe ten or twelve miles south, along the coast highway. I was supposed to start my investigation on the outskirts of a tourist town whose edges had gradually begun to house workers from elsewhere. Some actually had jobs back in the city; others didn't. The places I was supposed to visit were the usual spots: a couple of hotels, the campground, the police station, the restaurant, the gas station. Later I would probably visit other places. The sun beat on the car windows, unusual for October. But the air was cold and the highway was almost deserted. I drove past the first string of factories. Then an artillery barracks, through the open gates of which I could see a group of recruits smoking, their bearing far from military. Six miles further I entered a sort of forest broken up by houses and apartment buildings. I parked the car behind the campground and walked a while as I finished my cigarette, unsure of what to do. Two hundred yards away, just ahead of me, the train appeared. It was a blue train, four cars long at most. It was almost empty. I turned back. I sounded the horn several times but no one came to raise the barrier. The drive was gravel, shaded by tall pines; on either side there were tents and RVs camouflaged by the vegetation. I remember noting that it looked like the jungle, though I had never been in a jungle. At the end of the road, where it turned, something was moving, then a trash can came into view, wheeled along by an old man. I waved to him. At first he didn't seem to see me, then he came over, pulling the can after him with a look of resignation. I'm with the police, I said. He swore he had never seen the person I was looking for. Are you sure? I asked, handing him a cigarette. He said he was absolutely sure. It was more or less the same answer I got from everyone. Twilight found me in the car, parked on the Paseo Marítimo. I took out the instructions. The overhead light didn't work, so I had to use a cigarette lighter to read them. A couple of typewritten sheets with handwritten corrections. Nowhere did it say what I should be doing there. With those pages there were some black-and-white photos. I studied them carefully: it was the stretch of the Paseo Marítimo where I was now, maybe earlier in the day. "Our stories are sad, sergeant, there's no point trying to understand them" … "We've never hurt anyone" … "No point trying to understand them" … "The sea" … I balled up the papers and threw them out the window. In the rearview mirror I thought I could see how the wind swept them away. I turned on the radio, music, a program from the city; I switched it off. I lit a cigarette. I closed the window, still staring ahead, watching the lonely street and the boarded-up houses. I was struck by the idea of living in one of them during the winter season. They must be cheaper, I said to myself, unable to suppress a shiver.

13. THE BAR

The images set off down the road and yet they never get anywhere, they're simply lost, it's hopeless, says the voice—and
the hunchback asks himself, hopeless for who? The Roman
bridges are our fate now, thinks the author as the images
still shine, not too distant, like towns that the car gradually leaves behind. (But in this case the man isn't moving.) "I've made a count of airheads and severed heads" . . .
"There're definitely more severed heads" . . . "Although in
eternity it's hard to tell them apart" . . . I told a Jewish girl,
a friend of mine, that it was sad to spend hours in a bar listening to dirty stories. Nobody tried to change the subject.
Shit dripped from the sentences at breast height, so that I
couldn't stay seated, and I went up to the bar. Stories about
cops chasing immigrants. Nothing shocking, really, people
upset because they were out of work, etc. These are the sad
stories I have to tell you.

14. SHE HAD RED HAIR

I remember she moved from place to place without staying anywhere too long. Sometimes she had red hair, her eyes were green. The sergeant came up to her and asked for her papers. She turned to look at the mountains, it was raining there. She didn't talk much, most of the time she just listened to the conversations of the riders from the stable next door, or of the construction workers or the waiters from the restaurant on the highway. The sergeant avoided her eyes, I think he said it was too bad it was raining on the plain, then he pulled out a pack of cigarettes and offered her one. He was really looking for someone else, and he thought she might be able to give him some information. The girl watched the sunset, leaning on the riding school fence. The sergeant walked along a path in the grass, he had broad shoulders and was wearing a navy blue jacket. Slowly it began to rain. She closed her eyes when someone told her that he had dreamed of a corridor full of women without mouths; then she walked away toward the woods. An employee, a tired old man, turned out the lights at the riding school. With his sleeve he wiped the windowpanes. The policeman walked away without saying goodbye. In the dark, she took off her pants in the bedroom. She tried to decide on a corner, the hairs rising on the backs of her arms, and for a few moments she didn't move. The girl had witnessed a rape and the sergeant thought she could serve as witness. But he was really after something else. He put his cards on the table. Fade to black. In a leap he was standing on the bed. Through the dirty windows you could see the stars. I remember it was cold, a clear night. From where he stood the cop could see almost the whole riding school, the stables, the bar that was almost always closed, the rooms. She looked out the window and smiled. She heard footsteps coming up the stairs. The sergeant said she didn't have to talk if she didn't want to. "My links to the Body are almost nonexistent, especially from their own point of view" ... "I'm looking for someone who lived here a few seasons ago, I have reason to think you knew him" ... "Impossible to forget someone who looked like that" ... "I don't want to hurt you" ... "Along the coast they found golden woods and cabins vacant until next summer" ... "Paradise" ... "The redheaded girl watched the sun go down from the stable in flames" ...

15. THE SHEET

The Englishman said it wasn't worth it. For a long time he wondered what the Englishman meant. Ahead of him the shadow of a man slipped though the forest. He rubbed his knees but made no move to get up. The man popped up from behind a bush. Over his forearm, like a waiter approaching his first customer of the evening, he carried a white sheet. His movements were slightly clumsy and yet he radiated a serene authority when he walked. The hunchback assumed that the man had seen him. With a yellow cord the man tied a corner of the sheet to a pine, then tied the other corner to the branch of another tree. He repeated the operation with the bottom corners, after which the hunchback could only see his legs, because the rest of his body was hidden by the screen. The hunchback heard him cough. Then he came around the other side and contemplated the knots with which the sheet was tied to the pines. Not bad, said the hunchback, but the man ignored him. He reached his left hand up to the top left corner and slid it, the palm against the cloth, to the center. Once he had done that, he removed his hand and tapped the sheet a few times with his index finger to test the tension. He turned to face the hunchback and sighed in contentment. Then he clicked his tongue. His hair fell over his forehead, which was damp with sweat. He had a long red nose. Not bad, in fact, he said. I'm going to show a film. He smiled as if in apology. Before he left he looked up at the darkening treetops.

16. MY ONE TRUE LOVE

On the wall someone has written my one true love. She put the cigarette between her lips and waited for the man to light it for her. She was pale-skinned and freckled and had mahogany-colored hair. Someone opened the back door of the car and she got in silently. They glided along the deserted streets of a residential neighborhood. It was the time of year when most of the houses were empty. The man parked on a narrow street of single-story houses with identical yards. She went into the bathroom and he made coffee. The kitchen had brown tiles patterned with arabesques, and looked like a gym. She opened the curtains, there were no lights in any of the houses across the street. She took off her satin dress and the man lit another cigarette for her. Before she pulled down her underpants, the man arranged her on all fours on the soft white rug. She heard him look for something in the wardrobe. A wardrobe built into the wall, a red wardrobe. She watched him upside down, through her legs. The man smiled at her. Now someone is walking down a street where cars are parked only next to their respective lairs. Above the street, like a hanged man, swings the spotlit sign of the neighborhood's best restaurant, closed a long time ago. Footsteps vanish down the street, headlights are visible in the distance. She said no. She listens. There's someone outside. The man went over to the window, then came back naked toward the bed. She was freckled and sometimes she pretended to be asleep. He looked at her from the door with a kind of detached sweetness. There are silences made just for us. He pressed his face against hers until it hurt and pushed himself into her with a single thrust. Maybe she screamed a little. From the street, however, nothing could be heard. They fell asleep without moving apart. Someone walks away. We see his back, his dirty pants and his down-at-the-heel boots. He goes into a bar and settles himself at the counter as if he feels a prickling all over his body. His movements produce a vague, disturbing sensation in the other drinkers. Is this Barcelona? he asks. At night all the yards look alike, by day the impression is different, as if desires were channeled through the plants and flower beds and climbing vines. "They take good care of their cars and yards" ... "Someone has made a silence especially for us" ... "First he moved in and out and then in a circular motion" ... "Her buttocks were covered in scratches" ... "The moon is hiding behind the only tall building in the neighborhood" ... "Is this Barcelona?" ...

17. INTERVAL OF SILENCE

Look at these pictures, said the sergeant. The man who was sitting at the desk flipped through them indifferently. Do you think there's something here? The sergeant blinked with Shakespearean vigor. They were taken a long time ago, he started to say, probably with an old Soviet Zenith. Don't you see anything strange about them? The lieutenant closed his eyes, then lit a cigarette. I don't know what you're talking about. Look, said the voice … "A vacant lot at dusk" … "Long blurry beach" … "Sometimes you'd think he'd never used a camera before" … "Crumbling walls, dirty terrace, gravel path, a sign that says Office" … "A cement box by the side of the road" … "Restaurant windows, out of focus" … I don't know what the hell he's trying to get at. Through the window, the sergeant watched the train go by; it was so crowded there were even passengers on the roof. There're no people in them, he said. The door closes. A cop walks down a long, dimly lit hallway. He passes another cop with a file in his hand. They barely nod at each other. The cop opens the door of a dark room. He stands motionless inside the room, his back against the metal door. Look at these pictures, Lieutenant. It doesn't matter anymore. Look! Nothing matters anymore, go back to your office. "We've been consigned to an interval of silence." All I want is authorization to go back to the place where somebody took these pictures. Verbal authorization. Those cement boxes are for power lines, that's where the fuses go, maybe. I can find the shop where they were developed. This isn't Barcelona, says the voice. Through the foggy window he watched the train go by full of people. The woods are silhouetted against the light just so that half-closed eyes can enjoy the show. "I had a nightmare, and woke up when I fell out of bed, then I laughed at myself for almost ten minutes straight." There are at least two other cops who would recognize the hunchback, but they're away right now, on special assignments, worse luck. It doesn't matter anymore. In a small photo, black and white like all the rest, you can see the beach and a scrap of sea. Pretty fuzzy. There's something written in the sand. Maybe it's a name, maybe not, it might just be the photographer's footsteps.

18. THEY TALK BUT THEIR WORDS DON'T REGISTER

It's absurd to see an enchanted princess in every girl who walks by. What do you think you are, a troubadour? The skinny adolescent whistled in admiration. We were on the edge of the reservoir and the sky was very blue. A few fishermen were visible in the distance and smoke from a chimney rose over the trees. Green wood, for burning witches, said the old man, his lips hardly moving. The point is, there are all kinds of pretty girls in bed at this very moment with technocrats and executives. Five yards from me, a trout leaped. I put out my cigarette and closed my eyes. Close-up of a Mexican girl reading. She's blond, with a long nose and narrow lips. She looks up, turns toward the camera, smiles: streets damp after the rains of August, September, in a Mexico City that doesn't exist anymore. She walks down a residential street in a white coat and boots. With her index finger she presses the button for the elevator. The elevator arrives, she opens the door, selects the floor, and glances at herself in the mirror. Just for an instant. A man, thirty, sitting in a red armchair, watches her come in. He's dark-haired and he smiles at her. They talk but their words don't register on the soundtrack. Anyway, they must be saying things like how was your day, I'm tired, there's an avocado sandwich in the kitchen, thanks, thanks, a beer in the refrigerator. Outside it's raining. The room is cozy, with Mexican furniture and

Mexican rugs. The two of them are lying in bed. Small white flashes of lightning. Entwined and still, they look like exhausted children. Though they have no reason to be tired. The camera zooms out. Give me all the information in the world. A blue stripe splits the window in two halves. Like a blue hunchback? He's a bastard but he knows how to feign tenderness. He's a bastard but the hand on her side is gentle. Her face is buried between the pillow and her lover's neck. The camera zooms in: impassive faces that somehow, without intending to, shut you out. The author stares for a long time at the plaster masks, then covers his face. Fade to black. It's absurd to think that this is where all the pretty girls come from. Empty images follow one after the other: the reservoir and the woods, the cabin with a fire in the hearth, the lover in a red robe, the girl who turns and smiles at you. There's nothing diabolic about any of it. The wind tosses the neighborhood trees. A blue hunchback on the other side of the mirror? I don't know. A girl heads away, walking her motorcycle toward the end of the boulevard. If she keeps on in the same direction, she'll reach the sea. Soon she'll reach the sea.

19. ROMANCE NOVEL

I was silent for a moment and then I asked whether he really thought Roberto Bolaño had helped the hunchback just because years ago he was in love with a Mexican girl and the hunchback was Mexican too. Yes, said the guitarist, it sounds like a cheap romance novel, but I don't know how else to explain it, I mean in those days Bolaño wasn't overflowing with solidarity or desperation, two good reasons to help the Mexican. But nostalgia, on the other hand . . .

20. SYNOPSIS. THE WIND

Synopsis. The hunchback in the woods near the camp-ground and the tennis courts and the riding school. In Barcelona a South American is dying in a foul-smelling room. Police dragnets. Cops who fuck nameless girls. The English writer talks to the hunchback in the woods. Death throes and an asshole from South America, on the road. Five or six waiters return to the hotel along a deserted beach. Stirrings of fall. The wind whips up sand and buries them.

21. WHEN I WAS A BOY

Stray scenes kaput, long-haired kids on the beach again, but this time I might be dreaming—trees, dampness, paperbacks, slides at the end of which waits a little girl or a friend or a black car. I said wait for a movement of bodies, hairs, tattooed arms, choosing between prison and plastic (or aesthetic) surgery, I said don't wait for me. The hunchback cut out something that looked like a miniature poster and smiled at us from the branch of a pine tree. He was up in a tree, how long he'd been up there I don't know. "I can't get a fix on the frequencies of reality, they're so high" ... "A girl, motionless, who nonetheless spins, pinned to a bed that's pinned to the parquet that's pinned, etc." ... "When I was a boy I used to dream something like this ———~\/\/\WW\" ... "The straight line is the sea when it's calm, the wavy line is the sea with waves, and the jagged line is a storm" ... "I guess there isn't much aesthetics left in me" ... "nnnnnnn" ... "A little boat" ... "nnnnnnn" ... "nnnnnnn" ...

22. THE SEA

Photographs of the Castelldefels beach ... Photographs of the campground ... The polluted sea ... Mediterranean, October in Catalonia ... Alone ... The Zenith's eye ...

They alternated. The straight line made me feel calm.

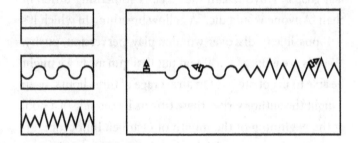

The wavy line made me uneasy, I sensed danger but I liked the smoothness: up and down. The last line was agitation. My penis hurt, my belly hurt, etc.

23. PERFECTION

Hamlet and *La Vita Nuova*, in both works there's a youthful breathing. For innocence, says the Englishman, read immaturity. On the screen there's only laughter, silent laughter that startles the spectator as if he were hearing his own last gasps. "Anyone can die" means something different than "Anyone would die." A callow breathing in which it's still possible to discover wonder, play, perversion, purity. "Words are empty" . . . "If you put that gun away we might be able to negotiate" . . . On an average of three hours' sleep a night the author writes these threats by the side of a pool at the beginning of the month of October. Innocence, almost like the image of Lola Muriel that I'd like to destroy. (But you can't destroy what you don't possess.) An urge, at the cost of nervous collapse in cheap rooms, propels poetry toward something that detectives call perfection. Dead-end street. A basement whose only virtue is its cleanliness. And yet who has been here if not *La Vita Nuova* and *Hamlet*. "I write by the pool at the campground, it's October, there are more and more flies now and fewer and fewer people; by the time we're halfway through the month there'll be no one left and the cleaning service will stop coming; the flies will take over until the end of the month, maybe."

24. FOOTSTEPS ON THE STAIRS

We came softly forward. The place in his memory that's labeled *immediate past* is furnished with mattresses scarcely touched by light. Gray mattresses with red and blue stripes in something that looks like a hallway or an overly long waiting room. In any case, his memory is frozen in *immediate past* like a faceless man in a dentist's chair. There are houses and streets that run down to the sea, dirty windows and shadows on staircase landings. We hear someone say "a long time ago it was noon," the light bounces off the center of *immediate past*, something that's neither a screen nor attempts to offer images. Memory slowly dictates soundless sentences. We imagine that all of this has been done to avoid confusion, a layer of white paint covers the film on the floor. *Fleeing together* long ago became *living together* and thus the integrity of the gesture was lost; the shine of *immediate past*. Are there really shadows on the landings? Was there really a hunchback who wrote happy poems? (Someone applauds.) "I knew it was them when I heard their footsteps on the stairs" . . . "I closed my eyes, the image of the gun didn't match the reality" . . . "I didn't bother to open the door for them" . . . "It was two in the morning and a blonde who looked like a man came in" . . . "Her eyes watched the moon through the curtain" . . . "A stupid smile spread slowly across her face daubed with white" . . . "The gun was only a word" . . . "Close the door, I said" . . . "Shattering isn't real, it's blackmail" . . .

25. TWENTY-SEVEN

The only possible scene is the one with the man on the path through the woods, running. Someone blinks a blue bedroom. Now he's twenty-seven and he gets on a bus. He's smoking a cigarette, has short hair, is wearing jeans, a dark shirt, a hooded jacket, boots, the dark glasses of a political commissar. He's sitting next to the window; beside him a workman on his way back from Andalusia. He gets on a train at the station in Zaragoza, he looks back, the mist has risen to the knees of a track worker. He smokes, coughs, rests his forehead on the bus window. Now he's walking around a strange city, a blue bag in his hand, his hood pulled up, it's cold, with each breath he expels a puff of smoke. The workman sleeps with his head resting on his shoulder. He lights a cigarette, glances at the plains, closes his eyes. The next scene is yellow and cold and on the soundtrack birds beat their wings. (He says: I'm a cage—it's a private joke—then he buys cigarettes and walks away from the camera.) He's sitting in a train station at dusk, he does a crossword puzzle, he reads the international news, he tracks the flight of a plane, he moistens his lips with his tongue. Someone coughs in the darkness, a cold clear morning from the window of a hotel; he coughs. He goes out to the street, pulls up the hood of his blue jacket, buttons all the buttons except the top one. He buys a pack of cigarettes, takes one, stops on the sidewalk by the window of a jewelry shop, lights a cigarette. He has short hair. He walks with his hands in the pockets of his jacket, the cigarette dangles from his lips. The scene is a close-up of the man with his forehead resting on the window. The rest is tiny passageways that hardly ever lead anywhere. The glass is foggy. Now he's twenty-seven and he gets off the bus. He heads down a deserted street.

26. AN EXTRA SILENCE

The fuzzy images of the hunchback and the policeman begin to retreat in opposite directions. The scene is black and liquid. In the space without memory a freshly shaven man with short hair appears. He's notable for his pallor and slowness. A voice says that the South American didn't die. (It's to be assumed that the figure who replaces the mist-hunchback and the mist-policeman is the South American.) He's wearing a navy blue jacket that calls to mind the last days of fall. Clearly he's been sick, his pallor and haggard face suggest as much. The screen splits down the middle, vertically. The South American walks along a deserted street. He recognizes the author and keeps walking. The screen recomposes itself as if it's just stopped raining. Sun-dappled gray buildings appear on an empty, familiar afternoon. The asphalt of the streets is clean and gray. The wind sweeps down avenues of red trees. Bright clouds are reflected in the windows of offices where no one is at work. Someone has created an extra silence. The mountain swoops at the end of the street. Little red-roofed houses scattered along the slope; thin spirals of smoke rise from some chimneys. Above is the reservoir, a lot for trucks, some makeshift latrines. In the distance a farmworker bends over the black earth. He's carrying a package wrapped in yellowed newspaper. The blurry heads of the hunchback and the policeman disappear. "The South American opened the door"... "All right, take him away"... "I don't know whether I'll be able to get in"...

27. OCCASIONALLY IT SHOOK

The nameless girl spread her legs under the sheets. A police-man can watch any way he wants, he's already overcome all the risks of the gaze. What I mean is, the drawer holds fear and photographs and men who can never be found, as well as papers. So the cop turned out the light and unzipped his fly. The girl closed her eyes when he turned her face down. She felt his pants against her buttocks and the metallic cold of the belt buckle. "There was once a word" . . . (Coughs) . . . "A word for all this" . . . "Now all I can say is: don't be afraid" . . . Images forced up by the piston. His fingers bur-rowed between her cheeks and she didn't say a thing, didn't even sigh. He was on his side, but she still had her head bur-ied in the sheets. His index and middle finger probed her ass, massaged her sphincter, and she opened her mouth with-out a sound. (I dreamed of a corridor full of people without mouths, he said, and the old man replied: don't be afraid.) He pushed his fingers all the way in, the girl moaned and raised her haunches, he felt the tips of his fingers brush something to which he instantly gave the name stalagmite. Then he thought it might be shit, but the color of the body that he was touching kept blazing green and white, like his first impression. The girl moaned hoarsely. The phrase "the nameless girl was lost in the metro" came to mind and he pulled his fingers out to the first joint. Then he sank them in again and with his free hand he touched the girl's forehead.

He worked his fingers in and out. As he squeezed the girl's temples, he thought that the fingers went in and out with no adornment, no literary rhetoric to give them any other sense than a couple of thick fingers buried in the ass of a nameless girl. The words came to a stop in the middle of a metro station. There was no one there. The policeman blinked. I guess the risk of the gaze was partly overcome by the exercise of his profession. The girl was sweating profusely and moved her legs with great care. Her ass was wet and occasionally quivered. Later he went over to look out the window and he ran his tongue over his teeth. (The word "teeth" slid across the glass, many times. The old man had coughed after he said don't be afraid.) Her hair spilled over the pillow. He mounted her, seemed to say something in her ear before he plunged into her. We knew he had done that by the girl's scream. The images travel in slow motion. He puts water on to boil. He closes the bathroom door. The bathroom light softly disappears. She's sitting in the kitchen, her elbows resting on her knees. She's smoking a cigarette. The policeman, the fake policeman, appears in a pair of green pajamas. From the hallway he calls her, asks her to come with him. She turns her head toward the door. There's no one there. She opens a kitchen drawer. Something gleams. She closes the door.

28. AN EMPTY PLACE NEAR HERE

"He had a white mustache, or maybe it was gray" ... "I was thinking about my situation, I was alone again and I was trying to understand why" ... "There's a skinny man over by the body now, taking pictures" ... "I know there's an empty place near here, but I don't know where" ...

29. YELLOW

The Englishman spotted him through the bushes. He walked away, treading on pine needles. It was probably eight o'clock and the sun was setting in the hills. The Englishman turned and said something to him but he couldn't hear a thing. It occurred to him that it had been days since he'd heard the crickets chirping. The Englishman moved his lips but all that reached him was the silence of the branches moving in the wind. He got up, his leg hurt, he felt for cigarettes in the pocket of his jacket. It was a denim jacket, old and faded. His pants were wide-legged and dark green. In the woods the Englishman moved his lips. He noticed that his eyes were closed. He looked at his fingernails: they were dirty. The Englishman's shirt was white and the pants he was wearing looked even older than his. The trunks of the pine trees were covered in brown scales, but when a ray of light fell on them they turned yellowish. In the distance, where the pines ended, there was an abandoned car motor and a few crumbling cement walls. His nails were big, and ragged because of his habit of biting them. He took out matches and lit a cigarette. The Englishman had opened his eyes. He flexed his leg and then smiled. Yellow. Flash of yellow. In the report he's described as a hunchbacked vagrant. For a few days, he lived in the woods. There was a campground nearby, but he didn't have enough money for that, so he only went every so often to the restaurant for a coffee. His tent was near the tennis and handball courts. Sometimes he went to watch people play. He came in through the back, through a gap the children had made in the tall grass. There's no information on the Englishman. Possibly he invented him.

30. THE MEDIC

An obsessive boy. Actually, what I mean is, if you knew him you couldn't stop thinking about him. The sergeant went up to the fallen shape in the park. He noticed people looking out their windows. Behind him came the medic's footsteps. He lit a cigarette. The medic blinked and asked if they could finally take the fucking body away. He yawned, putting out the match. "I have no idea what city I'm in" ... "It's always the picture of that idiot boy on the screen" ... "Always clowning on the brim of hell" ... "Always tapping my shoulder with his skinny fingers to ask if he can come in" ... The medic spat. He felt like farting. Instead, he knelt by the body. People, undressed, leaning on their elbows in the dark windows. It had been a while since they felt any real sense of danger. The writer, I think he was English, confessed to the hunchback how hard it was for him to write. All I can come up with are stray sentences, he said, maybe because reality seems to me like a swarm of stray sentences. Desolation must be something like that, said the hunchback. "All right, take him away" ...

31. A WHITE HANDKERCHIEF

I'm walking in the park, it's fall, looks like somebody got killed. Until yesterday I thought my life could be different, I was in love, etc. I stop by the fountain, it's dark, the surface shiny, but when I brush it with the palm of my hand I feel how rough it really is. From here I watch an old cop approach the body with hesitant steps. A cold breeze is blowing, raising goose bumps. The cop kneels by the body: with a dejected gesture, he covers his eyes with his left hand. A flock of starlings rise. They circle over the policeman's head and then disappear. The policeman goes through the dead man's pockets and piles what he finds on a white handkerchief that he's spread out on the grass. Dark green grass that seems to want to swallow up the white square. Maybe it's the dark old papers that the cop sets on the handkerchief that make me think this way. I decide to sit down for a while. The park benches are white with black wrought-iron legs. A police car comes down the street. It stops. Two cops get out. One of them heads toward where the old cop is crouched, the other waits by the car and lights a cigarette. A while later an ambulance silently appears and parks behind the police car. "I didn't see anything" ... "A dead man in the park" ... "An old cop" ...

32. CALLE TALLERS

He used to make the rounds of the old city of Barcelona. He wore a long shabby trench coat, smelled of black tobacco, and almost always happened upon the most unusual scenes a few minutes in advance. In other words, the screen flashed the word "unusual" to make him appear. "I'd like to have a word with you in private," he'd say. The street parallel to the Paseo Marítimo of Castelldefels. A workman walks along the sidewalk, hands in his pockets, rhythmically masticating a cigarette. Empty houses, the wooden shutters closed. "Take off your clothes slowly, I won't look." The screen opens like a mollusk. I remember a while ago reading the pronouncements of an English writer who said how hard it was for him to keep his verb tenses consistent. He used the word "suffer" to give a sense of his struggles. Under the trench coat there's nothing, perhaps the faint whiff of a hunchback lost in contemplation of the Jewish girl, of trashed apartments on Calle Tallers (skinny Alan Monardes stumbles down the dark hallway), of heroes of winters that gradually fade into the past. "But you write, Montserrat, and you'll get through this." He removed his coat, took her by the shoulders, and then hit her. Her dress dropped in slow motion onto her fur coat. Just like that she got down on all fours and offered him her rear. I saw it all from the next room through the hole someone had drilled for that purpose. He rubbed his flaccid penis on her buttocks. Carelessly he glanced to one side: rain was sliding down the window. The screen flashes the word "nerve." Then "grove." Then "deserted." Then the door closes.

33. THE REDHEAD

She was eighteen and she was mixed up in the drug trade. Back then I saw her all the time but if I had to make a police sketch of her now, I don't think I could. I know she had an aquiline nose, and for a few months she was a redhead; I know I heard her laugh once or twice from the window of a restaurant as I was waiting for a taxi or just walking past in the rain. She was eighteen and once every two weeks she went to bed with a cop from the Narcotics Squad. In my dreams she wears jeans and a black sweater, and the few times she turns to look at me she laughs a dumb laugh. The cop would get her down on all fours and kneel by the outlet. The vibrator was dead but he'd rigged it to work on electric current. The sun filters through the green of the curtains, she's asleep with her tights around her ankles, face down, her hair covering her face. In the next scene I see her in the bathroom, looking in the mirror, then she says good morning and smiles. She was a sweet girl and she didn't avoid certain obligations: I mean sometimes she might try to cheer you up or loan you money. The cop had a huge dick, at least three inches longer than the dildo, and he hardly ever fucked her with it. I guess that's how he liked it. He stared with teary eyes at his erect cock. She watched him from the bed . . . She smoked Camel Lights and maybe at some point she imagined that the furniture in the room and even her lover were empty things that she had to invest with meaning . . .

Purple-tinted scene: before she pulls down her tights, she tells him about her day . . . "Everything is disgustingly still, frozen somewhere in the air." Hotel room lamp. A stenciled pattern, dark green. Frayed rug. Girl on all fours who moans as the vibrator enters her cunt. She had long legs and she was eighteen, in those days she was in the drug trade and she was doing all right, she even opened a checking account and bought a motorcycle. It may seem strange but I never wanted to sleep with her. Someone applauds from a dark corner. The policeman would snuggle up beside her and take her hands. Then he would guide them to his crotch and she could spend an hour or two getting him off. That winter she wore a red knee-length wool coat. My voice fades, splinters. She was just a sad girl, I think, lost now among the multitudes. She looked in the mirror and asked, "Did you do anything nice today?" The cop from Narcotics walks away down an avenue of larches. His eyes were cold, sometimes I saw him in my dreams sitting in the waiting room of a bus station. Loneliness is an aspect of natural human egotism. One day the person you love will say she doesn't love you and you won't understand. It happened to me. I would've liked her to tell me how to endure her absence. She didn't say anything. Only the inventors survive. In my dream, a skinny old bum comes up to the policeman to ask for a light. When the policeman reaches into his pocket for a lighter the bum sticks him with a knife. The cop falls without a sound. (I'm sitting very still in my room in Distrito V, all that moves is my arm to raise a cigarette to my lips.) Now it's her turn to be lost. Adolescent faces stream by in the car's rearview mirror. A nervous tic. Fissure, half saliva, half coffee, in the bottom lip. The redhead walks her motorcycle away down a tree-lined street . . . "Disgustingly still" . . . "She says to the fog: it's all right, I'm staying with you" . . .

34. LAUNCH RAMPS

It's a scene of squares, nothing else. They sit on the screen all day, like a still photograph. It gets dark. In the distance there's a cluster of houses with smoke beginning to trickle from the chimneys. The houses are in a valley surrounded by brown hills. The squares grow damp. From their edges seeps a kind of cartilaginous sweat. Now it's definitely night; at the foot of one of the hills a workman buries a package wrapped in newspaper. We can see the article: in a suburb of Barcelona there's a playground as dangerous as a mine-field. In one of the photographs that accompany the story, a slide is visible a few yards from an abyss; two children with goose bumps wave from the top of the slide. Back to the squares. The surface has changed into something that vaguely reminds us, like Rorschach blots, of offices in a police station. From the desks a drooling man, breathing with difficulty, stares at the squares, trying to recognize the houses, the hills, the footsteps of the workman fading into the brown and sepia darkness. Now the squares flicker. A plainclothes policeman walks down a narrow, deserted hallway. He opens a door. Before him spreads a landscape of launch ramps. The policeman's footsteps echo in the silent yard. The door closes.

35. A HOSPITAL

The girl weighs 60 pounds now. She's in the hospital and it seems she's losing ground. "Destroy your stray phrases." I didn't understand what she meant until much later. Doubt was cast on my honesty, my reliability: they said I slept while I was on guard duty. Really, they were after someone else and I happened to show up at the wrong time. The girl weighs 60 pounds now and she probably won't leave the hospital alive. (Someone applauds. The hallway is full of people who open their mouths without a sound.) A girl I knew? I don't remember anyone with that face, I said. On the screen there's a street, a drunk kid is about to cross, a bus appears. The prompter said, "Sara Bendeman?" Still, I couldn't understand anything at the time. All I remember is a skinny girl with long freckled legs, undressing at the foot of the bed. The scene continues in a dimly lit alley: a woman, forty, smokes a cigarette on the fourth floor, leaning on the windowsill. Up the stairs comes a panting cop in civilian clothes, his features like mine if I'd overdosed on cortisone. (The one person who applauded closes his eyes now. In his mind something takes shape, something that might be a hospital if the meaning of life were different. In one of the rooms the girl is in bed. The curtains are open and light spills into the room.) "Destroy your stray phrases" . . . "A policeman climbs the stairs" . . . "In his gaze there is no hunchback, no Jewish girl, no traitor" . . . "But we can still insist" . . .

36. PEOPLE WALKING AWAY

Nothing lasts, the purely loving gestures of children tumble into the void. I wrote: "a group of waiters returning to work" and "windswept sand" and "the dirty windowpanes of September." Now I can turn my back on him. The hunchback is your guiding light. White houses scattered across the mountainside. Deserted highways, the screech of birds in the trees. And did I do everything? did I kiss her when she'd stopped expecting kisses? (Miles from here people are applauding, and that's why I feel such despair.) Yesterday I dreamed that I lived inside a hollow tree—soon the tree began to spin like a carousel and I felt as if the walls were closing in on me; I woke to find the door of the bungalow ajar. The hunchback's face shone in the moonlight . . . "Lonely words, people walking away from the camera, and children like hollow trees" . . . "No matter where you go" . . . I stopped at the fucking "lonely words." Undisciplined writing. It was forty men, more or less, all working for starvation wages. Each morning the Andalusian laughed uproariously when he read the paper. Waxing moon in August. In September I'll be alone. In October and November I'll pick pineapples.

37. THREE YEARS

The only rule that exists is a redheaded girl watching us from the end of the fence. Bruno understood this the same way I did, he just cared about different things. The cops are tired, there's a gasoline shortage, and thousands of unemployed youths roam Barcelona. (Bruno is in Paris, playing sax outside the Pompidou, they say, and without a girlfriend now.) With oily steps, four or five waiters approach the shack where they sleep. One of them used to write poetry, but that was a long time ago. The author said: "I can't be pessimistic or optimistic, everything is determined by the beat of hope that manifests itself in what we call reality." I can't be a science fiction writer because my innocence is mostly gone and I'm not crazy yet . . . Words that no one speaks, that no one is required to speak . . . Hands in the process of geometric fragmentation: writing that's stolen away just as love, friendship, and the recurring backyards of nightmares are stolen away . . . Sometimes I get the sense that it's all "internal" . . . Maybe that's why I lived alone and did nothing for three years . . . (The man hardly ever washed, he didn't need a typewriter, all he had to do was sit in that shabby armchair for things to flee of their own accord) . . . A surprising evening for the hunchback? Policemen's faces an inch from his nose? Did the rain really wash clean the windowpanes?

38. THE GUN TO HIS MOUTH

Screen of blond hair. Behind it the hunchback draws swimming pools, commuter towns, empty streets. Tact or courtesy stems from proper behavior in each situation. The hunchback draws a person with a kind face. "I lay there on my back in bed, I heard the crickets chirp and someone recite Manrique." Under the parched trees of August, I write to understand stillness, not to please. A kind person! Whether it's art or a five-minute adventure of a boy running up some stairs. "My departure escaped the author's eye." An ah, and an oh, and postcards from whitewashed towns. The hunchback strolls down the empty pool, sits in the deep end, and lights a cigarette. The shadow of a cloud passes, a spider pauses next to his fingernail, he expels smoke. "Reality is a drag." I suppose all the movies I've seen will be worth nothing to me when I die. Wrong. They'll be worth something, believe me. Don't stop going to the movies. Scene of an empty commuter town, old newspapers blowing in the wind, dust crusted on benches and restaurants. I have long had this war inside me, which is why it doesn't affect me internally, wrote Klee. Was it in Mexico City that I saw the hunchback for the first time? Was it Gaspar who told stories about cops and robbers? They put the gun to his mouth and pinched his nose ... He had to open his mouth to breathe and then they shoved the barrel in ... In the center of the black curtain there's a red circle ... I think the man said shit or mama, I don't know ...

39. BIG SILVER WAVES

The foreigner stayed here. That tent you see there was his tent. Go on in. He spent a long time under that tree, thinking, though it looked like he was dead. From where we're standing you could see his face covered in sweat. Big drops formed on his chin and dripped onto the grass. Here, feel, he slept for hours in the weeds here, like a dead man. The guy came into the bar and had a beer. He paid with French money and put the change in his pocket, not counting it. He spoke perfect Spanish. He had a camera that the police took as evidence. He walked on the beach in the evening. In this scene, the beach looks pale, pale yellow, with fading golden splotches. He dropped onto the sand, like a dead man. The only soundtrack was the dry obsessive cough of someone we could never see. Big silver waves, the guy standing on the beach, barefoot, and the cough. A long time ago were you happy in a tent too? In some corner of his memory there's a scene where he's on top of a thin brown girl. It's nighttime in a deserted campground, somewhere in Portugal. The girl is on her stomach and he moves in and out of her, biting her neck. Then he turns her over. He lifts her legs onto his shoulders and both of them come. An hour later he's on top of her again. (Or as a Conde del Asalto pimp says: "wham bam wham bam times infinity.") I don't know whether I'm talking about the same person. His camera is in some evidence locker now and maybe no one's thought to develop the film. Endless hallways, nightmarish, along which strides a fat tech from the Homicide Squad. The red light is off now, you can come in. The policeman's face relaxes into a smile. From the end of the hallway the silhouette of another policeman approaches. He crosses the space that separates him from his colleague and then both of them disappear. Empty now, the gray of the hallway quivers or maybe it swells. Then the silhouette of a policeman appears at the other end. He advances until he's in the foreground, pauses. In the background another cop appears. The shadow moves toward the shadow of the cop in the foreground. Both disappear. The smile of a tech from the Homicide Squad keeps watch over these scenes. Fat cheeks drenched in sweat. There's nothing in the photographs. (A stifled attempt at applause.) Nothing we can see. "Call someone, do something" . . . "A fucking cough echoing across the beach" . . . "The tent full of spiderwebs" . . . "Everything is wrecked" . . . "Faces, stray scenes, kaput" . . .

40. THE MOTORCYCLISTS

Imagine the situation: the nameless girl hiding on the landing—it's an old building, poorly lit, with an open-grille elevator. Behind the door a man of about forty whispers, in a confessional tone, that he, too, is being chased by Colan Yar. The brown-and-black opening shot vanishes almost instantly, giving way to a deep panorama—stores with multicolored roofs. Then: dark green trees. Then: red sky with clouds. Was a kid asleep in the tent just then? Dreaming of Colan Yar, police cars parked in front of a smoldering building, twenty-year-old criminals? "All the shit in the world," or: "A campground should be the closest thing to Purgatory," etc. With dry, trembling hands he pushed back the curtains. Below, the motorcyclists revved their engines and took off. He whispered "very far away" and clenched his teeth. Fat blondes—young women from Andalusia confident of their appeal—and among them the nameless girl, with her guillotine mouth, strolling through the past and the future like a movie face. I imagined my body tossed away in the countryside, just a few yards from the town's first houses. A camper, out for a walk, found me, he was the one who alerted the police. Now, under the cloudy sky, I'm surrounded by men in blue and white uniforms. The guardia civil and tabloid photographers, or maybe just tourists whose hobby is taking pictures of dead bodies. Gawkers and children. It isn't Paradise, but it's close. The girl goes slowly down the stairs. I opened the office door and ran downstairs. On the walls I saw furious whales, an incomprehensible alphabet. The street noise woke me up. On the opposite sidewalk a man yelled and then wept until the police came. "A body just outside of town" . . . "The motorcyclists are lost on the highway" . . . "No one will ever close this window again" . . .

41. THE BUM

I remember one night at the Merida train station. My girlfriend was asleep in her sleeping bag and I was keeping
watch with a knife in the pocket of my jacket. I didn't feel
like reading. Anyway . . . Phrases appeared, I mean, I never
closed my eyes or made an effort to think, the phrases
just appeared, literally, like glowing ads in the middle of
the empty waiting room. Across the room, on the floor,
slept a bum, and next to me slept my girlfriend, and I was
the only one awake in the whole silent, repulsive Merida
train station. My girlfriend breathed calmly in her red
sleeping bag and that calmed me. The bum sometimes
snored, sometimes talked in his sleep, he hadn't shaved
for days, and he was using his jacket as a pillow. His left
hand shielded his chest. The phrases appeared like news
on an electronic ticker. White letters, not very bright, in
the middle of the waiting room. The bum's shoes stood
next to his head. The toe of one of his socks was full
of holes. Sometimes my girlfriend shifted. The door to
the street was yellow and in some places the paint had
a bleak look. I mean, only slightly, but at the same time
absolutely bleak. I wondered whether the bum was dangerous. Phrases. I clutched the knife, still in my pocket,
and waited for the next phrase. In the distance I heard the
whistle of a train and the ticking of the station clock. I'm

saved, I thought. We were on our way to Portugal, and this happened some time ago. My girlfriend breathed. The bum offered me cognac from a bottle he had in his bag. We talked for a few minutes and then we were quiet until morning.

42. CLEAR WATER ALONG THE WAY

What's yet to come. The wind in the trees. Everything is the projection of a forlorn kid. He's walking alone along a back road. His mouth moves. I saw a group of people opening their mouths, unable to speak. The rain filters through the pine needles. Someone is running in the woods. You can't see his face. Just his back. Pure violence. (In this scene the author appears with his hands on his hips watching something offscreen.) The wind and the rain through the trees, like a curtain of madmen. The wind blows like a ghost on a deserted beach: lifts his pajamas, pushes him across the sand until he disappears in the middle of an asthma attack or a long yawn. "Like a rocket sliced open" . . . "The poetic way of saying that you no longer love back streets lit up by patrol cars" . . . "The melodic voice of the sergeant speaking with a Galician accent" . . . "Boys your age who'd settle for so little" . . . "It's too bad" . . . "There's a kind of dance that turns into lips" . . . Wells of clear water along the way. You saw a man on the ground under the trees and you kept running. The first wild blackberries of the season. Like the screwed-up eyes of the excitement that rushed to meet you.

43. LIKE A WALTZ

In the railroad car a girl on her own. She looks out the window. Outside everything splits in two: tilled fields, woods, white houses, towns, suburbs, dumps, factories, dogs, and children waving goodbye. Lola Muriel appears. August 1980. I dream of faces that open their mouths and can't speak. They try but they can't. Their blue eyes stare at me but they can't. Then I walk along the corridor of a hotel. I wake up sweating. Lola has blue eyes and she reads Poe stories by the pool, while the other girls talk about pyramids and jungles. I dream that I'm watching it rain in neighborhoods which I recognize but have never visited. I walk along an empty passageway. I see faces with eyes that close and mouths that open, though they can't speak. I wake up sweating. August 1980? A girl, eighteen, from Andalusia? The night watchman, madly in love?

44. NEVER ALONE AGAIN

Silence hovers in the yards, leaving no pages with writing on them, that thing we'll later call the work. Silence reads letters sitting on a balcony. Birds like a rasp in the throat, like women with deep voices. I no longer ask for all the loneliness of love or the tranquility of love or for the mirrors. Silence glimmers in the empty hallways, on the radios no one listens to anymore. Silence is love just as your raspy voice is a bird. And no work could justify the slowness of movements and obstacles. I wrote "a nameless girl," I saw a radio by the window and a girl sitting on a chair and in a train. The girl was tied up and the train was in motion. The folding of wings. Everything is a folding of wings and silence, from the fat girl afraid to get in the pool to the hunchback. Her hand turned off the radio . . . "I've seen some happy marriages—the silence builds a kind of double victory—foggy windowpanes and names written with a finger" . . . "Maybe dates, not names" . . . "In the winter" . . . Scene of policemen rushing into a gray building, sound of gunfire, radios turned all the way up. Fade to black. The tenderness of an old whore and her cloak of silvery silence. And I no longer ask for all the solitude in the world, but for time. They shoot. Phrases like "I've lost even my sense of humor," "so many nights alone," etc., remind me of the meaning of retreat, a folding inward. Nothing's written. The foreigner, motionless, imagines that this is death. The hunchback trembles in the empty pool. I've found a bridge in the woods. Lightning flash of blue eyes and blond hair . . . "For a while, never alone again" . . .

45. APPLAUSE

She said she loved busy days. I looked up at the sky. "Busy days," and also insects and clouds that drift down to the bushes. This flowerpot I leave in the country is proof of my love for you. Then I came back with my butterfly net in the fog. The girl said: "calamity," "horses," "rockets sliced open," and turned her back on me. Her back spoke. Like the chirping of crickets in the afternoons of lonely houses. I closed my eyes, the brakes squealed, and the policemen leaped out of their cars. "Keep looking out the window." Without any explanation, two of them came to the door and said "police," the rest I could hardly hear. I closed my eyes, crickets chirped, the boys died on the beach. Bodies riddled with holes. The brakes squealed and the cops got out. There's something obscene about this, said the medic when nobody was listening. I'll probably never come back to the clearing in the woods, not with flowers, not with the net, not with a fucking book to spend the afternoon. His mouth opened but the author couldn't hear a thing. He thought about the silence and then he thought "there's no such thing," "horses," "waning August moon." Someone applauded from the void. I said I guessed this was happiness.

46. THE DANCE

On the terrace of the bar only three girls are dancing. Two are thin and have long hair. The other is fat, with shorter hair, and she's retarded ... The guy being chased by Colan Yar vanished like a mosquito in winter ... Though really, I guess in the winter all that's left are the mosquito eggs ... Three happy, hardworking girls ... August 7, 1980 ... The guy opened the door to his room, turned on the light ... There was an expression of horror on his face ... He turned out the light ... Don't be afraid, though the only stories I have to tell you are sad, don't be afraid ...

47. THERE ARE NO RULES

Big mistakes. Nameless girl returning to the scene of the deserted campground. Deserted bar, deserted reception area, deserted plots. This is your Wild West ghost town. She said: in the end they'll destroy us all. (Even the pretty girls?) I laughed at her despondence. Doubly afraid of himself because he couldn't help falling in love once a year at least. Then a succession of porta-potties, cheap reprints, kids puking, while a retarded girl dances on the silent terrace. All writing on the edge hides a white mask. That's all. There's always a fucking mask. The rest: poor Bolaño writing at a pit stop. "Police cars with their radios on: useless information raining down on them from all the neighborhoods they pass through." "Anonymous letters, subtle threats, the real wait." "My dear, now I live in a tourist town, the people are tan, it's sunny every day, etc." There are no rules. ("Tell that stupid Arnold Bennet that all his rules about plot only apply to novels that are copies of other novels.") And so on and so on. I, too, am fleeing Colan Yar. I've worked with retarded people, at a campground, picking pineapples, harvesting crops, unloading ships. Everything drove me toward this place, this vacant lot where nothing remains to be said . . . "At least you're with beautiful girls" . . . "I'd say the only beautiful thing here is the language" . . . "I mean it in the most literal way" . . . (Applause.)

48. LA PAVA ROADSIDE BAR OF CASTELLDEFELS

(Everyone's Eaten More Than One Dish or One Dish Costing More Than 200 Pesetas, Except for Me!)

Dear Lisa, once I talked to you on the phone for more than an hour without realizing that you had hung up. I was at a public phone on Calle Bucareli, at the Reloj Chino corner. Now I'm in a bar on the Catalan coast, my throat hurts, and I'm close to broke. The Italian girl said she was going back to Milan to work, even if it made her sick. I don't know whether she was quoting Pavese or she really didn't feel like going back. I think I'll go to the campground nurse for some antibiotics. The scene breaks up geometrically. We see a deserted beach at eight o'clock, tall orange clouds; in the distance a group of five people walk away from the observer in Indian file. The wind lifts a curtain of sand and covers them.

49. ANTWERP

In Antwerp a man was killed when his car was run over by a truck full of pigs. Lots of the pigs died too when the truck overturned, others had to be put out of their misery by the side of the road, and others took off as fast as they could . . . "That's right, honey, he's dead, the pigs ran right over him" . . . "At night, on the dark highways of Belgium or Catalonia" . . . "We talked for hours in a bar on Las Ramblas, it was summer and she talked as if she hadn't talked for a long time" . . . "When she was done, she felt my face like a blind woman" . . . "The pigs squealed" . . . "She said I want to be alone and even though I was drunk I understood" . . . "I don't know, it's something like the full moon, girls who are really like flies, though that's not what I mean" . . . "Pigs howling in the middle of the highway, wounded or rushing away from the smashed-up truck" . . . "Every word is useless, every sentence, every phone conversation" . . . "She said she wanted to be alone" . . . I wanted to be alone too. In Antwerp or Barcelona. The moon. Animals fleeing. Highway accident. Fear.

50. SUMMER

There's a secret sickness called Lisa. Like all sicknesses, it's miserable and it comes on at night. In the weave of a mysterious language whose words signify without exception that the foreigner "isn't well." And somehow I would like her to know that the foreigner is "struggling," "in strange lands," "without much chance of writing epic poetry," "without much chance of anything." The sickness takes me to strange and frozen bathrooms where the plumbing works according to an unexpected mechanism. Bathrooms, dreams, long hair flying out the window to the sea. The sickness is a wake. (The author appears shirtless, in black glasses, posing with a dog and a backpack in the summer somewhere.) "The summer somewhere," sentences lacking in tranquility, though the image they refract is motionless, like a coffin in the lens of a still camera. The writer is a dirty man, with his shirt sleeves rolled up and his short hair wet with sweat, hauling barrels of garbage. He's also a waiter who watches himself filming as he walks along a deserted beach, on his way back to the hotel . . . "The wind whips grains of sand" . . . "Without much chance" . . . The sickness is to sit at the base of the lighthouse staring into nothing. The lighthouse is black, the sea is black, the writer's jacket is also black.

51. YOU CAN'T GO BACK

You can't go back. This world of cops and robbers and foreigners without papers is too powerful for you. Powerful means it's comfortable, a featherweight world, without entropy, a world you know and from which you're never able to remove yourself. Like a tattoo. In exchange, however, you'd get back your native land, and the laws that protect you, and the right to meet a very beautiful girl with a dumb voice. A girl standing in the door to your room, the maid who's come to make your bed. I stopped at the word "bed" and closed the notebook. All I had the strength to do was turn out the light and fall into "bed." Immediately I began to dream about a window with a heavy wooden frame, carved like the ones in children's book illustrations. I shoved the window with my shoulder and it opened. Outside there was no one. A silent night in the blocks of bungalows. The policeman showed his badge, trying not to stutter. Car with a Madrid license plate. The man on the passenger side was wearing a T-shirt with the Barcelona colors, the stripes horizontal instead of vertical. An indelible tattoo on his left arm. Behind them gleamed a mass of fog and sleep. But the cop stuttered and I smiled. You c-c-can't g-g-go b-b-back. Go back.

52. MONTY ALEXANDER

That's the way it is, he said, a slight sense of failure that keeps growing stronger and the body gets used to it. You can't escape the void, just as you can't help crossing streets if you live in a city, with the added annoyance that sometimes the street is endlessly wide, the buildings look like warehouses out of gangster movies, and some people choose the worst moments to think about their mothers. "Gangsters" equals "mothers." At the golden hour, no one remembered the hunchback. "That's the Way It Is," the name of a piece by Monty Alexander recorded in the early 1960s at an L.A. club. Maybe "warehouses" equals "mothers," a wide margin of error is permissible when you're dealing with superimpositions. All thought is registered on the path through the woods along which the foreigner walked back and forth. If you saw him from above you'd think he was a solitary ant. Flash of doubt: there's always another ant that the camera doesn't see. What poems lack is characters who lie in wait for the reader. "Warehouses," "gangsters," "mothers," "forever." His voice was hard, he said, solid in timbre like the collapse of a cattle hoist or a hay bale in a cattle pond. He drooled as he spoke, some sentences were riddles that no one bothered to decipher. Ray Brown on bass, Milt Jackson on vibraphone, and two others on sax and drums. Monty Alexander himself played piano. Manne-Hole, 1961? The last thing he saw was the beach at nine o'clock. In July it got dark very late, at nine-thirty it was still light out. A group of waiters moving away from the eye. (But the eye envisions "warehouses," not "waiters.") The wind lifts soft curtains of sand. From here, it looks like they'll try to come back.

53. WORKING-CLASS NEIGHBORHOODS

The nameless girl wanders the working-class neighborhoods of Barcelona. A girl born in France, to Spanish parents? The beach stretches in a straight line to the next town. She opened the window, it was overcast but hot. She went back into the bathroom. She gazed curiously at the buildings along the street. All of this is paranoia, she thought. She's eighteen but she doesn't exist, she was born in an industrial city of France and her name is Rosario or María Dolores, but she can't exist because I'm still here. The guard is asleep? She checked her watch. Returning to the window, she lit a cigarette. Through the curtains the boys dozed amid the shadows on the street. Intermittent forms, the sound of barely audible voices. She stared at the moon that hung over the building across the street. From the street came the words "ship," "Olympia," "restaurant." The girl sat on the terrace of a "restaurant" and asked for a glass of white wine. Over her head was the green awning, and, above that, the summer. Like the moon peeping over the building and her gazing at it, thinking about the motorcyclists and the name of the month: July. Born in France to Spanish parents, blond hair, very far away from the restaurant and the words with which they try to distract her. "I woke up because you were lost in the shadows of the bedroom" . . . "A powerful explosion" . . . "I was deaf for the rest of the day" . . . She dreamed of empty cars in lots as black as coal. There are no more towns or working-class neighborhoods for this actor. Eighteen years old, so far away. She goes back into the bathroom. Girl kaput.

54. THE ELEMENTS

Movies under the pines at the Estrella de Mar campground. The spectators watch the screen and slap at mosquitoes. A yellow face suddenly appears among the rocks and asks: are you, too, being chased by Colan Yar? (Yellow face crisscrossed with broad dark scars, burned trees, white plastic chairs left in front of the bungalows, a bicycle in the weeds.) Colan Yar, of course, and plaques faintly lit by the moon. I left my post; with slow steps I headed to the restaurant, which was still open at this late hour. "Colan Yar after me, right on my heels," I heard people saying behind my back. When I turned all I could see were the shapes of trees and dark tents. In the movie one of the actors said "We're being chased by a volcano." Another character, a woman, at some point observed: "It's no easy thing to become a major in the English army." Chased by the Nagas, diabolical warriors in black leather helmets, worshippers of the volcano, maybe priests, not warriors; in any case, soon wiped out. The actress: "I'm tired of fighting these awful creatures." An actor says: "Do you want me to carry you to the plane?" Five figures flee through a valley in flames. An Armada icebreaker waiting for them at 20:30 hours, not a minute later. The captain: "If we stay, we won't be able to get out later." The captain's hair is completely white and he's wearing a blue winter uniform. He enunciates slowly: "We won't be able to get out." I glanced away from the screen. From the distance the tennis court lights made it look like a secret airfield. Back there, the person fleeing Colan Yar writes a letter sitting on a bench outside. Secret airfield. Mirrors. Other elements.

55. NAGAS

Movies in the woods? The projectionist naps on a lounge chair in the backyard of his bungalow. The nameless girl disappeared as meekly as the first time I saw her. I walked forward unafraid, leaving faint footprints in the dust. It was midnight and I saw police cars pulled over on the highway. I didn't answer Mara's last letter. The girl walked back to her tent and no one could say whether she'd come out or not. The next morning she was gone. "I've written all I can" . . . "A ten-year-old girl is the only one left, she waves to me whenever she sees me" . . . "She sat alone on the terrace of the bar, next to the dance floor, and she wasn't hard to find" . . . On the screen, the Nagas appear. Spectators and a cloud of mosquitoes. I glanced to the right: distant lights of the tennis courts. I felt like falling asleep right there. These are the elements: "impassivity," "perseverance," "blond hair." The next morning she was no longer in her tent. Along the death-doomed European highways her parents' car glides. On the way to Lyon, Geneva, Bruges? On the way to Antwerp? He looked around wearily: waxing moon, the crowns of pine trees silhouetted against the sky, the sound of sirens in the distance. But I'm safe here, he said, the killer didn't recognize me and he's gone. Black-and-white scene of a man who heads into the woods after the screening. Final images of adults napping as a strange car moves to encounter a greater brightness.

56. POSTSCRIPT

Of what is lost, irretrievably lost, all I wish to recover is the daily availability of my writing, lines capable of grasping me by the hair and lifting me up when I'm at the end of my strength. (Significant, said the foreigner.) Odes to the human and the divine. Let my writing be like the verses by Leopardi that Daniel Biga recited on a Nordic bridge to gird himself with courage.

BARCELONA 1980